D1455738

Do Something in Your State

Amanda Rondeau

Consulting Editor, Diane Craig, M.A./Reading Specialist

ABDO
Publishing Company

Published by ABDO Publishing Company, 4940 Viking Drive, Edina, Minnesota 55435.

Copyright © 2004 by Abdo Consulting Group, Inc. International copyrights reserved in all countries. No part of this book may be reproduced in any form without written permission from the publisher. SandCastle™ is a trademark and logo of ABDO Publishing Company.

Printed in the United States.

Credits
Edited by: Pam Price
Curriculum Coordinator: Nancy Tuminelly
Cover and Interior Design and Production: Mighty Media
Photo Credits: Corbis Images, Comstock, Digital Vision, PhotoDisc, Rubberball Productions, Skjold Photography

Library of Congress Cataloging-in-Publication Data

Rondeau, Amanda, 1974-.
    Do something in your state / Amanda Rondeau.
    p. cm.--(Do something about it!)
    Includes index.
    ISBN 1-59197-575-1
    1. Child volunteers--Juvenile literature. 2. Social action--Juvenile literature. 3. Community development--Juvenile literature. 4. Quality of life--Juvenile literature. I. Title. II. Series.

    HQ784.V64 R663 2004
    361--dc21
                                                                    2003058389

SandCastle™ books are created by a professional team of educators, reading specialists, and content developers around five essential components that include phonemic awareness, phonics, vocabulary, text comprehension, and fluency. All books are written, reviewed, and leveled for guided reading, early intervention reading, and Accelerated Reader® programs and designed for use in shared, guided, and independent reading and writing activities to support a balanced approach to literacy instruction.

Let Us Know

After reading the book, SandCastle would like you to tell us your stories about reading. What is your favorite page? Was there something hard that you needed help with? Share the ups and downs of learning to read. We want to hear from you! To get posted on the ABDO Publishing Company Web site, send us e-mail at:

sandcastle@abdopub.com

SandCastle Level: Transitional

You can make a difference in your state by doing something to make it a better place to live.

When you do something to help others, you are making a difference.

Mr. Zane wants to uphold laws and teach people about safety.

He became a state trooper.

Ms. Meyer loved going to camp when she was young.

She is a camp counselor and makes camp fun for kids.

Ms. Miller thinks it's important to learn about history.

She makes history fun by being a guide at a history museum.

Mr. Ruiz worries about people without homes.

He volunteers to help build houses for people who need them.

Mia and Lori love to go to state parks.

They help keep the trails neat by clearing away the leaves.

Jim likes to build things with wood.

He and his mom make birdhouses and donate them to parks.

Bill helps with a statewide drive for kids without toys.

He helps sort the toys after school.

Recycling
PICK-UP
MONDAY

SAINT
PAUL

Neighbors Working Together

Mindy teaches other kids about recycling.

Recycling saves her state money and is good for the environment.

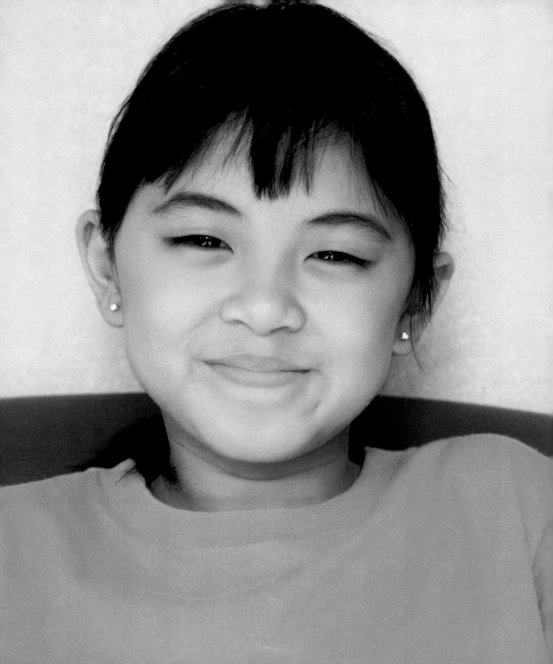

There are many ways you can make a difference in your state.

What would you like to do?

Glossary

birdhouse. a box provided for birds to nest in

camp. a place, usually in the country, with tents or cabins where people go for fun and learning

counselor. a person who gives advice to others

donate. to give a gift to charity

drive. an organized effort to do something

environment. nature and everything in it, like the land, sea, and air

guide. a person or thing that tells how to get around and explains interesting things

history. things that happened in the past

law. a rule that is made by the government and must be obeyed

museum. a place where artistic, scientific, or historic things are cared for, studied, and displayed

recycle. to process something so the materials it is made of can be used again

trooper. a police officer hired by the state to enforce its laws

volunteer. to offer to do a job, most often without pay

About SandCastle™

A professional team of educators, reading specialists, and content developers created the SandCastle™ series to support young readers as they develop reading skills and strategies and increase their general knowledge. The SandCastle™ series has four levels that correspond to early literacy development in young children. The levels are provided to help teachers and parents select the appropriate books for young readers.

Emerging Readers
(no flags)

Beginning Readers
(1 flag)

Transitional Readers
(2 flags)

Fluent Readers
(3 flags)

These levels are meant only as a guide. All levels are subject to change.

ABDO
Publishing Company

To see a complete list of SandCastle™ books and other nonfiction titles from ABDO Publishing Company, visit www.abdopub.com or contact us at:
4940 Viking Drive, Edina, Minnesota 55435 • 1-800-800-1312 • fax: 1-952-831-1632